EARTH INVADERS
Operation 27

Written by Brittany Lindsey
Illustrated by Samantha Woods

Dedicated to my son, the light of my life and my husband, the one who gives me the world.

A portion of all proceeds of this book will be donated to *FK (Foster Kids) Your Diet* in relief efforts for the Fort Myers, Florida community after the effects of Hurricane Ian (2022).

Printed in the United States of America
First Printing, 2023
ISBN 9798395282934

CHAPTER 1

September 30th, 2022

Drifting along the Milky Way on an extraterrestrial space station lives a humble alien society, the Plutonians. Throughout the galaxies the Plutonians are recognized for their kind and inquisitive nature. With their history recorded and celebrated for over a millenia, this alien society overflows with intelligence. Then there's Cosmo, a 4th grade Plutonian with a different view of the galaxy. Intelligent?

Without a doubt. Inquisitive? Absolutely. Kind?
Questionable.

Two words.

World Domination. These two words are the constant song that plays in Cosmo T. Lunar's ever so intelligent mind.

"Muahahaha, MUAHAHAHA It's happening, it's really HAPPENING! It's so close I can taste it... world domination!" cackled Cosmo so powerfully that you could hear it from the next universe, "everything is going according to plan."

"What do you mean 'going according to the plan?', we haven't even decided on the plan yet," replied Nova with a galactic eye roll.

Cosmo quickly replied, "Oh... right...well, I forgot to tell you guys. We *do* have a new plan and it's been masterminded by none other than the evil genius that is me, obviously, and it's so utterly perfect that I could

4

shed a tear," gabbed Cosmo as he dramatically sniffed back a nonexistent tear. "I feel it in my bones. The sun, the stars, the planets, EVERYTHING is aligned. *Nothing* is going to get in our way. Total world domination... here I... I mean we...come."

"Dun dun DUUUUUUN," chirped Neb.

"That's what you said last time...and the time before that... and the time before that..." mocked Nova, "what makes this time any different?"

"*This tim*e is different, Nova," Cosmo responded while sticking his tongue out, " because I've found it! I've searched and scoured the big blue and green planet and I've finally found the ideal location for us to build our take-over-the-planet lair. Once we've built our lair, we will be *unstoppable*. What makes this the prime location you may ask? This location is secluded, truly hidden from sight. It's moderate in temperature. The sun shines there year round meaning we would never have to worry about that frozen white stuff that falls from the sky and best of all? The location is a mere eighteen feet away from the Gulf of Mexico, which is ideal for a quick escape, should something go wrong. If this spot doesn't scream **world domination,** I don't know what does!" Cosmo panted from talking so quickly, trying to catch his breath. "Cometta, activate operation 27 location data," ordered Cosmo.

"Aroo. Activating operation 27 location data," barked Cometta as she projected four pictures, all different angles of a pristine beach with an inconspicuously abandoned wooden hut craftily tucked away within the towering Bermudagrass, onto the wall of the space station's common room. Bottle Palm Trees filled with green coconuts, sand as glittery white as the stars, and a crystal clear sea dancing in the sunshine. The three aliens gawked at the stunning pictures. Nova studied each one closely. Neb's eyes grew bright with excitement. Cosmo darted up to the projection and slapped a red x-marks-the-spot sticker in the middle of the second photo.

"Right…here!" he howled as he leapt to reach the picture. "This is what we've been searching for! X marks the spot of our brand new hideout and I, being as brilliant as I am, already instructed Cometta to transport my Travel Technology System and a few other necessities. She shipped it a few hours ago and has since received confirmation that it landed safely next to the wooden hideout hut. It will be waiting there for us once we arrive. No need for applause, I already know how awesome this is, " Cosmo beamed as he patted his own back boastfully.

"It looks nice I guess. Really 'take-over-the-worldy'," Nova replied, "but where on Plutonia is this place exactly?"

Cosmo's grin grew wider than the Milky Way. "Pack your take-over-the-world kits and your jammies! WORLD DOMINATION here we come! We're going to… take it away, Cometta."

Cometta beeped. "Aroo. Coordinance 26°
21' 5.301" N 81° 51' 18.317" W. Bonita Beach,
Florida."

"Oh Em Gee! Bonita BEACH?! I *love*
the beach! There are so many cute little
Earthlings there getting all tan and sandy. Let's
go, let's go, let's GO!" celebrated Neb as he
raced to pack his T.O.T.W. kit and jammies.
The three Plutonians packed their
astrobags as fast as the speed of light, launched
themselves into their spaceship; the Star Blaster
500, and set their sights on the big blue and
green planet; Earth.

~

"T.O.T.W. kits?" questioned Nova with a
tilt of her pen.
"Check," replied Neb.
"Astrobags?"

"Check."

"Earthling camouflage?"

"Check."

"Travel Technology System," continued Nova.

"Uh… uhm no it's not" Neb started to say as he was interrupted by Cosmo.

"The T.T.S. is already on location waiting for us, remember?" butted in Cosmo.

"Right… let's just hope no one bothers it before we get there," cautioned Nova.

"You saw how inconspicuous the wooden hut was. Who would think to check on it?" challenged Cosmo.

"You've got a point there, Cos," agreed Neb.

"Alright, that's everything on our checklist. The Starblaster 500 has everything else we could possibly need. I think we're ready for takeoff. Cosmo, take it away," instructed

Nova as she carefully placed the checklist back inside of her astrobag.

"Cometta, activate launch system," directed Cosmo.

"Aroo, activating launch system. 3... 2... 1... take off initiated," barked Cometta.

"Hey Neb, what's in your T.O.T.W. kit anyway?" questioned Nova.

"Oh uh, just some things that...we really might... you know what? It's nothing. Really, it's nothing," mumbled Neb with a cheeky smile as he checked to make sure all of his astronaut snacks and his Earthling plushie were still safely packed away.

Ah yes, and so it begins. The three young Plutonian's latest quest for world domination. It seems like absolutely nothing could go wrong... Or could it?

CHAPTER 2

Space travel isn't for the faint of heart, but for the three young and determined Plutonians, it was the perfect napping condition… indicated by the echoing snores and three massive piles of drool.

"Aroo, initiating landing gear," barked Cometta. The landing gear on the Star Blaster 500 jetted out centimeters away from the toasty white sand with a rattling so intense that it shook the young trio awake. Nova and Neb yawned sleepy yawns while Cosmo rubbed his eyes as they adjusted to the golden sun shining through the window of his spacecraft.

"We made it! WORLD DOMINATION here we come! Would you just look at that sun!" celebrated Cosmo with a quirky little dance.

"Alright gang, let's prepare to survey the area. We have a great deal of groundwork to begin if we're going to take over Earth. Cometta, gather our T.O.T.W. kits and begin transporting them to… " Nova began to say, but was cut off as Neb let out a galactic sized wail.

"WHAT… HAPPENED?!" sobbed Neb, "The little wooden hut…the beach… everything… it's all ruined!"

Fallen trees, collapsed fences, and a splintered wooden disaster where the charming beach hut used to stand was all the Plutonians could see. The same question was on everyone's mind. What on Earth happened here?

"Way to go, Cosmo," mocked Nova with one of her famous eye rolls. "Were the pictures Cometta showed us from a hundred years ago or something?"

"What?! NO! At least I don't think so..." defended Cosmo. "Cometta, activate operation 27 location data. Let's check the timestamp on those photos."

"Aroo, activating operation 27 location data," beeped Cometta. A glowing hologram of pictures beamed out of Cometta's eyes. The friends gathered around the hologram and studied the photographs silently.

"But… but this doesn't make any sense. These photos were taken on September 27th, 2022. That's only three days ago. What on Plutonia could have possibly happened to this poor beach in just three days?" questioned Nova as tears began welling.

Out of the corner of her eye, she saw something yellow fluttering in the wind. She turned without muttering a word and walked towards a yellow tape tied to a broken fence post near the entrance to the beach. She grabbed the torn yellow tape that read 'caution', turned back to her friends, and motioned for them to follow.

"This is caution tape," Nova informed her friends, "during my research in Professor

Gorb's Earth History class last month I learned that Earthlings use this tape to warn each other about imposing danger. What could have been so dangerous that it could do this," Nova waved her hand back toward the beach that was in ruins, "to such a beautiful beach?"

To Cosmo's dismay, world domination quickly left the trio's mind as they realized how devastating this situation truly was. How could they take over Earth if they didn't know what could be there lurking around the corner to stop them?

"Do… do you think we should check on the cute little Earthlings? Maybe talk to some of 'em? Whatever has done this, they should be able to tell us, right?" suggested Neb as he thought fondly of his beloved humans. "I love those little guys."

"Professor Gorb warned us about talking to the Earthlings, Neb," reminded Nova.

"You're right, but Professor Gorb also said not to talk to Earthlings *unless* it was absolutely necessary and this," Neb motioned back to the destroyed beach, "this seems pretty important to me."

Obvious tension started to build between Neb and Nova. "Neb's right. We can't take over the Earth without knowing everything we can about this planet. Especially something so dangerous that it can cause this level of destruction in such a short time. Cosmetta, activate the Star Blaster 500's invisibility shield and retrieve our Earthling Camouflage, pronto!" commanded Cosmo.

"Aroo, activating the Star Blaster 500's invisibility shield. Earthling Camouflage in 3..2..1..." beeped Cometta. Three bundles tied neatly in a bow launched from the cargo compartment and landed on the sand next to the aliens with a thud.

"That's what I'm talkin' about. Thanks Cometta!" expressed Cosmo. The Plutonian trio eagerly grabbed the Earthling Camouflage; a pair of dark sunglasses and a white 'I love Florida' beach t-shirt, and changed quicker than a shooting star.

CHAPTER 3

The young Plutonians and Cometta
cautiously shuffled their way up the mangled
boardwalk while searching the barren streets for
any sign of Earthlings. The beach town was
demolished. Every pastel colored building for
miles had plywood boards tacked on to guard
their windows. It was clear that the Earthlings
were trying hard to protect themselves and their
town… but from what? Trees seemed to be
carelessly thrown everywhere. Doors were
busted in and the exposed building materials

were swollen with what seemed like water. The trio continued on their search for any sign of humans, but it seemed like a lost cause. Not only was the beach town destroyed, it was also deserted.

All of a sudden the group was stopped in their tracks at a haunting sight. They stood in front of a disheveled light pink building. The sign, which was sideways and hanging on by a single wire, read Bonita Beach Treasures. From the outside looking in, it was clear that this was the ghost of a once prominent beach themed gift shop. Sand littered the floor of the gift shop and the shelves that were once filled with beachy trinkets had collapsed onto themselves, ruining the souvenirs as they fell. Everything was waterlogged. Nova mindfully stepped over the scattered debris and entered the shop. Neb and Cosmo followed closely behind her.

"Look over at the wall next to the shattered window," Nova directed as she climbed over a soaking wet ceiling tile that was now in a broken, sopping heap on the floor. " Watch your step. There's broken glass on the floor here," she paused and pointed, "do you see that?"

"See what?" asked Cosmo.

"That!" Nova pointed towards the far side of the shop. "Look at this line. It's a line made of debris and do you notice anything peculiar? If you look around at the entirety of the building, the line is at the same exact height on every interior wall. The wallpaper is tattered and destroyed below the debris line, but the decor above the line seems untouched. It's almost as if the ocean was inside this shop and stopped right below this line. Cometta, scan this room and record the damage. Add the information to our Operation 27 data," instructed Nova.

"Aroo," responded Cometta as a bright red laser scanned the devastated interior of

Bonita Beach Treasures, "data cataloged within Operation 27."

"How on Earth would the ocean get inside a building? That doesn't make any sense," Cosmo thought out loud.

"I don't know guys, this is pretty freaky. I think we should get out of here. We've got some cute little Earthlings to find, remember?" reminded Neb. The Plutonians silently agreed and ever so cautiously made their trek back through the disheveled gift shop.

Cosmo and Neb were the first to make it out of Bonita Beach Treasures, but as Nova climbed through the rubble, something dainty caught her eye. She dug one hand through a small pile of wreckage while bracing herself on a broken chair with the other, desperately trying not to slip. The object was shoved below a broken picture frame and when Nova finally dislodged it, she smiled. She held a petite, sparkly conch shell with two googly eyes and the words 'Bonita Beach, FL' on its back. This shell seemed to be the sole survivor of whatever horror this shop went through and Nova didn't have the heart to leave it there. She wiped the dirt away and tucked her new little friend in the zipper pocket of her astrobag while she cautiously made her way out of Bonita Beach Treasures.

CHAPTER 4

Cosmo, Neb, Nova and Cometta stood
on a jagged sidewalk and peered out to the
seemingly deserted beach town. The amount of
destruction was unlike anything any of the
young Plutonians had ever seen before. Finding
an Earthling in this mess seemed impossible
when they couldn't even locate a building that
was fully intact and unscathed. Worry was
oozing out of the three friends, but
determination was Cosmo's most notable trait.
Nothing was going to stop him from figuring

out what had happened to this town in such a short amount of time.

Cometta's ears perked as she caught the faint sound of Earthling communication coming from the next street over.

"Aroo, multiple Earthings detected fifty three feet ahead. Continue with caution," beeped Cometta. Instantly, the trio pivoted in pursuit.

"Let me do the talkin' guys. Earthlings are my specialty. Ooh I just can't wait to talk to them," squeaked Neb, "and remember, we are incognito. We ARE one with the Earthlings. Heck, just call me Neb the human! Just play it cool."

"I don't think *we* are the ones who need to be reminded to 'play it cool', Neb," scoffed Nova.

"Just act natural, don't overthink it, Neb," reminded Cosmo.

Just as they turned the corner to make their way down the next street, Neb broke out into a full on sprint. Cosmo's and Nova's eyes were as big as a full moon with an unspoken 'uh oh!' ringing between them. The pair and Cometta quickly chased after him in hopes of catching up quickly.

While panting and trying to catch his breath, Neb approached the group of Earthlings. As soon as the humans noticed Neb, who was still out of breath, they took a break from cleaning up the rubble on the street outside of a home with a missing roof and began speaking as Nova, Cosmo, and Cometta ran up to the group.

"Hey you! You all need to be careful. Would you just take a look around? There's broken glass, down power lines, and hazards everywhere you step down here. It's definitely not a safe place to walk your dog," warned the elder Earthling who was wearing a special outfit and a badge that read Sheriff.

"Yeah," Nova chimed in, "we noticed!" She whipped out her galactic notebook and scribbled down the word 'sheriff'. She had never heard that name before, but she thought it sounded really out-of-this-world. She noted that it was the perfect name for her new little shell friend. Neb's eyes grew wider than an asteroid belt and his cheeks flushed as pink as the walls of the Bonita Beach Treasures gift shop. His shyness took over and he just couldn't seem to find his voice. The Earthling, Sheriff, started walking away to return to the seemingly endless clean up. As he turned, he was stopped by Cosmo's hand grabbing onto his arm. Sheriff halted and faced him. Cosmo quickly glanced at the others and then back at the Earthling.

"What… what happened here?" Cosmo's voice shook with concern. The three Plutonians and Cometta waited anxiously for the

Earthling's answer. The Sheriff was silent for what seemed like eons. It was so quiet, you could hear a pin drop on the moon.

"You kids didn't hear? Did you watch the news at all last week? It's all anyone could talk about. *It* made landfall on our beach. *Its* winds were so forceful that it sounded like trains driving by our windows. *Its* storm surge was horrifying; causing flooded streets, businesses, and houses. The poor Bonita Beach Treasures gift shop had seven feet of sea water within its walls. That's even taller than me!" cried the Earthling. The trio stood in silent shock as Sheriff continued. "Boats, cars, and even the pier were thrown by the winds and carried away by the surge. I didn't believe my eyes at first, but I actually saw a sailboat on top of my neighbors' house! In my twenty two years of service, this was like nothing I have witnessed before."

"But what is *'it'*? Was it an asteroid? A massive moon monster? Maybe a black hole?" rattled off Nova.

The Earthling scowled. He was still for a moment, looking out to the ocean that was so close you could taste the seasalt. Minutes passed and finally he spoke.

"Hurricane Evan."

The Plutonians looked around at each other, clearly confused. They had completed countless hours of research in Professor Gorb's Earth History class, and yet none of them had ever heard of Hurricane Evan.

"So... it was a monster, huh? I knew it! Wow, a real moon monster. Do you know where it was going? Why was it on a rampage? Was it going through a feeding frenzy?" Nova sputtered out question after question until the Earthling interrupted.

"A monster? No. Well, at least not the *live under your bed* kind anyway. You three really have never heard of a hurricane? Where did y'all say you were from? Canada?" questioned the Sheriff, puzzled, "You're definitely not from here with *those* t-shirts."

"Note to the file- invest in better Earthling camouflage," Cosmo whispered to Cometta.

"Aroo, copy that… I mean woof," beeped Cometta.

"Wait a second, did that dog just… never mind, I must be hearing things. I'm exhausted from this whole ordeal. I'd say it's just about time you guys head back and find your parents. They must be worried sick about you out here. I wish you safe travels back up to Canada. It must be pretty snowy there, definitely a lot colder than it gets here in Florida," piped the Earthling.

Just as the Sheriff turned to continue his clean up, Neb finally found his voice. "Earthl- I mean, Sheriff… Thank you for taking the time to talk with us today. You've given us a lot to think about. One last thing before we go if you wouldn't mind of course. Would you take a picture with me? PLEASEEE!" begged Neb.

"Erm… sure," muttered the sheriff, still rather confused at this whole interaction, "I guess this was a vacation you'll never want to forget. Might as well remember it with a selfie next to all the wreckage."

Neb threw his arm around the sheriff and squeezed him tightly in a big hug. His toothy smile shone brighter than the North Star. Cometta accessed her camera feature and snapped a polaroid picture of Neb and the Earthling before the human could understand what she was doing. The polaroid sputtered out of Cometta's mouth, fully developed. Earthling was fully perplexed.

"Thanks again for all of your information. It will be very useful once we get back to... What did you call it? Oh right... 'Canada'," said Cosmo while trying to stay serious and hide his grin.

"Did that dog just print a picture from her... you know what? Never mind.." The Sheriff scratched his head feeling dizzy from this conversation as he finally was able to return to his debris pile.

The Plutonians and Cometta started making the short journey back to the Star Blaster 500. Nova was scribbling away in her galactic notebook. All of this talk of surges, train sounding winds, Hurricane Evan, and Canada had her mind moving a million light years a minute. So many questions were swirling in her head. She longed to find the answers but wasn't quite sure where to start.

Frustration was oozing throughout Cosmo's brilliant mind. Yet again, his plans of World Domination had been foiled and this time by something he didn't even understand. Worst of all, the group's Travel Technology System was somewhere deep in the Gulf of Mexico being tossed around by dolphins. His dreams of becoming the fearsome supreme leader of Earth seemed to be weightless as it floated farther and farther away.

CHAPTER 5

October 1st, 2022

"Aroo, activating landing gear in
3...2...1..." Cometta barked as the Starblaster
500's landing gear jetted out right as it touched
down on the space station's landing strip.

"Smooth sailing as always Cometta,
interstellar work! Here girl, want a bolt?"
Cosmo chirped as he tossed his robodog her
favorite snack. Cometta crunched away on the
bolt as she rolled into her dog chargehouse to

recharge after another long, unsuccessful trip to the big blue and green planet.

"Well, what do we do now?" pondered Cosmo.

"You know… I know… Neb knows…. We all know what we have to do now, don't we?" remarked Nova, a little annoyed with having to remind Cosmo again as if they don't always have an end of mission assessment to make. Cosmo hung his head in defeat and slowly nodded.

"Yeah… I guess I do," Cosmo sighed, "Neb, want to do the honors?"

"Uhm. ABSOLUTELY!" Neb replied cheerfully as if he didn't even realize that their plan had been foiled yet again. "Look on the bright side, Cos, at least we still have each other. That's really all that matters!" Neb carefully opened his astrobag and retrieved his new polaroid of himself and Sheriff hugging next to a collapsed wall. Ever so carefully, Neb took a thumbtack and placed the photo on the huge white wall of the common room next to twenty six other pictures. He placed his hands on his waist and grinned at his handiwork. Nova slid up next to him and placed an index card below the polaroid with a caption that read, *Operation 27: Unsuccessful. Cause: Hurricane Evan.*

Cosmo stared at the pictures on the wall, feeling defeated and a bit heavy. Twenty seven photos now represented the twenty seven failed attempts at World Domination. Twenty seven failed attempts at accomplishing his dream.

Just as the trio began to unpack their astrobags, the common room door creaked open as quietly as a Haley's Comet. As the door silently opened, a towering purple creature with eight sticky tentacles slithered across the floor. The creature was slithering closer and closer to the group, utterly undetected.

"Ahh! Oh gosh. I didn't see ya there.
You scared me half to death! How are you, Sir?
Long time no see!" Neb sputtered out as he
embraced this giant purple creature in a warm
hug, a Neb specialty.

"Professor Gorb! Just the Plutonian we
needed to talk to. We just descended back to the
station from our trip to the big blue and green
planet and came across some unsettling news
that has us questioning everything we've ever

learned in your class!" Cosmo eagerly informed the Professor.

"It's as clear as Saturn's Rings that your latest quest for World Domination wasn't quite the triumph you insisted it would be. Questions hmm? Let me grab my monocle," grunted Professor Gorb as he rummaged through his tote bag until he found his golden monocle, a status symbol of intelligence for the Plutonians. With a slimy pop, he unstuck the monocle from the sucker on his tentacle and carefully placed it on his one, rather large eyeball. "Ah yes, that's better, alright. Let's hear it. What circumstances resulted in this unsuccessful attempt?"

"We had the perfect plan. Absolutely nothing was supposed to go wrong. It was the optimal time of year. I identified a prime location for our lair. The stars could not have been more aligned and yet, we were faced with something that left total destruction in its wake. The beach was pristine when I logged all of my information on it, but when we arrived it was decimated. The hideout hut crumbled into a pile of sticks. All of my precious technology had been washed away to sea," Cosmo sniffed back a tear, " Everything. EVERY LITTLE THING that could have gone wrong DID go wrong!" He wailed a little over dramatically.

"Okay Cosmo," Nova huffed with an eye roll greater than the Big Dipper, "Let me cut to the chase, Professor. One day electronic photos were uploaded to Cometta's Earth Database of a normal, secluded beach and within a matter of three days, it was unrecognizable. We did some digging to try to get to the bottom of what could have happened and we realized that not only was our beach hut kaput, but the little town of Bonita Beach had faced a real life monster that left a path of broken trees, flooded shops, and destroyed buildings. We decided to go against your cautions and found an elder Earthling. Sheriff gave this faceless monster a name;

Hurricane Evan," she shuddered as she spoke its name.

"Have you heard of this infamous Hurricane Evan, Prof?" wondered Neb. "My heart hurts for those adorable little humans who have to repair so much of their community. I just want to hug every single one of them."

Professor Gorb smiled at him. "That's momentously empathetic of you, Neb, and while no, I've never studied Hurricane Evan per say, I have done research on hurricanes just like it," Professor Gorb said with a twist of his monocle.

"You mean to tell me that there are MORE of these monsters?!" shouted Cosmo, positively puzzled.

"Oh yes, indeed. Statistically speaking, hurricanes occur multiple times a year and in multiple locations on Earth," Professor Gorb muttered as he began rummaging through his seemingly bottomless tote bag, yet again. "Ah, yes here it is. I knew this would come in handy one of these days." Stuck to his sticky suction cups was a black, bulky hardcover textbook titled *Extreme Weather Patterns of Earth.*

"Well, we better get started then, Professor. We have so many questions for you to answer about the hurri…" Cosmo began to exclaim when he jumped with surprise and was interrupted by a booming thud that was loud enough to wake the sleeping Gas Giants. The weather textbook slipped and un-suctioned itself from Professor Gorb as it clammored to the table.

"Questions… questions indeed. I must admit, I do indeed have extensive knowledge about Earth's weather, and yet simply telling you the answers is no fun, no fun at all. Better yet, I challenge you all. I challenge you all to use this resource and uncover all of your own wonderings. Ask yourselves your questions, use your big, beautiful brains and some helpful chapters of my book, and then use the details you uncover to spread your new found knowledge to your classmates. On Monday, the floor of our classroom will be yours," the Professor challenged.

"UGH RESEARCH?!?" whined Cosmo. Neb and Nova's smiles stretched from antenna to antenna.

"Challenge totally accepted!" cheered Neb.

"RESEARCH?! I LOVE RESEARCH!" squealed Nova, sounding more like Neb than her usual sarcastic self.

"What a wonderfully illuminating day Monday will be for all of us! With that, my comrades, I bid you adieu."

With a tip of his cap, Professor Gorb wriggled his way back to the common room door with a little pop pop pop that sounded exactly like wet bubble wrap crunching every time he lifted his tentacles to take another step.

Professor Gorb had entrusted the young Plutonians with a substantial mission that would not only help enlighten Cosmo, Nova, and Neb, but also the entire 4th grade Plutonian population. The trio had the guidance of Professor Gorb and now understood that Hurricane Evan wasn't a real life monster with a fancy name, but was merely one of the countless hurricanes that occur annually and in a multitude of areas on Earth. But, what on Plutonia is a hurricane?

Cosmo, not overly thrilled about the research part of this challenge, was as hungry as ever for World Domination. He shortly realized that once he was able to fully understand what happened to foil his latest plan to overthrow Earth, he would be better suited to start preparation for his next quest for total world domination. Like a lightswitch, his sad, defeated demeanor became a knowledge hungry determination and the Cosmo that Neb and Nova came to love was back and ready to tackle the mission at hand.

"Soon friends, SOON!" howled Cosmo, "utter world domination will be back within our grasps. Listen up gang, it's time to get to work. Nova, you're on hurricane research. We will need you to gather every last detail there is in the Earth Database on hurricanes. Here," Cosmo tossed the heavy black textbook at

Nova, not very gently. "Knowing professor Gorb, everything you'll need will be within those pages."

"On it, Captain," saluted Nova.

"Neb, you're on Earthling Impact. We need to understand how humans combat these so-called monsters," Cosmo directed.

"You got it Cos, I LOVE those Earthlings. Best task everrrr!" beamed Neb with a galactic grin and a high five so encouraging that it stung Cosmo's palm and left it tingling as Neb sprinted out of the room back to his sleeping quarters.

"Cometta, activate operation 27 location data and cross reference the Plutonian National Earth Database. We're going to unearth the **big** questions. The fastest, the largest, the most dangerous. That's on us!"

"Aroo!" beeped Cometta.

With the mission clear in their minds, the trio and Cometta dispersed to their own quarters of the space station and eagerly got down to business. Keyboards clacking, pencils scribbling, and Cosmo diabolically cackling every few minutes was all that could be heard. The Plutonians had two days to prepare for Monday's presentation. And prepare they did.

CHAPTER 6

October 3rd, 2022

Dawn broke on an overly anticipated Monday morning. Neb slinked out of his restpod, glanced at the poster the trio had assembled and worked tirelessly on for the last two days, and felt the room begin to spin. Neb loved everyone; from his teacher to his classmates, and yet he had a dizzying fear of public speaking. He felt his fear start bubbling to the surface trying to take over, but today meant so much to him. Neb turned and stared at the reflectionator on his door, took a big, deep belly breath, and looked directly into his own eyes. "Nebulous, you've totally got this! You are intelligent. You are a kind friend. You are brave. You can do hard things, even if it's a little intimidating. I KNOW you can do this!" If no one else, Neb was going to be his own biggest supporter. He wasn't going to let anything, especially himself, stop him from illuminating his classmates about something that had affected his beloved Earthlings. He was filled with too much pride to let anything get in his way.

Chapter 7

The Plutonian Academy of Excellence is nestled away in the westernmost point of the space station. Through the towering double paned doors lives the hustle and bustle of the most notable Plutonians that rival even Professor Gorb's vast intelligence. A multitude of learning rooms line the halls. These halls are home to extensive extraterrestrial research, astrophysical experiments, and collaboration across the galaxies. It's also where the youngest members of the Plutonian society learn from the greatest minds about their infinite history and today, they'd be learning from Cosmo, Nova, and Neb.

"Good morning, my brilliant students! I hope you all had an eventful long holiday weekend and were able to get outside to celebrate Plant a Plorg day. On my way into school today, I wandered through Plutonian National Park and noticed all the freshly planted plorgs. I was even able to pluck this off one for my breakfast," the Professor proudly held up his shiny, red plaple for his students to admire.

"Ah yes, today, my young scholars, today is a very special day indeed. We are all in for an extraterrestrial treat. Today, I am going to be stepping down from my podium and you, my dear students, will have the honor of learning from three of your very own. To put it short, Cosmo, Neb, and Nova had quite the interesting trip to the big blue and green planet and encountered something that I know will have your bright minds buzzing. Without further adieu, I ask you three to take your rightful place at the front of our classroom." Professor Gorb slithered to the empty desk towards the back of the classroom and suctioned onto his seat. The trio gathered their materials and made their way up to the front of the room.

"Close your eyes and imagine a tropical paradise. Can you see it? A beautiful beach with powdery white sand, crystal clear ocean water, and the sky as blue as Ultra Blue stars. Sounds pretty perfect right? Yeah, that's what we thought too. Cometta, activate Operation 27 Location Data September 27th, 2022. Cosmo directed his peers to the projection of Bonita Beach, the exact same photo that he was so eager to show Neb and Nova just a few short days ago.

Oohs and ahhs rang out all around the room. "How delightful!" eagerly whispered

Constella, one of the 4th grade Plutonians, "I just love the big blue and green planet!"

"You're right, it was beautiful," replied Cosmo, "a perfect spot for world dom… err a much needed vacation…"

"So perfect in fact, we three decided to make the trek to the big blue and green planet and see this little spot for ourselves. We were so totally stoked. That is… until we landed," added Neb. Cometta turned off her projector accessory and the "before" photo of Bonita Beach faded away. The room became nearly too dark to see.

"Our mini tropical vacation took a turn that we never saw coming," Cosmo began, "Cometta, activate location 27 location data September 30th, 2022.

"Aroo," barked Cometta. The class was fidgety with anticipation. The new projection of Bonita Beach was shocking to say the least.

Some classmates gasped, while others were shocked into silence.

"The picture perfect piece of paradise was nowhere in sight," Nova continued as her words cut the silence in the classroom like an astroblade. "When we landed, we were dismayed. We scoured the area for any clues we could have possibly gathered, but it seemed as if a monster had made its way to this beachtown and went on a destructive rampage. I mean, what else could have possibly left a place like this in total ruins in a matter of days?"

"I'll tell you what could cause this much destruction. It in fact, was not a monster. It was an extreme storm called Hurricane Evan," informed Cosmo, "and no, it's not the only one of its kind. Our research has shown us that these extreme weather occurrences, called hurricanes, happen multiple times a year on Earth and we are here today to teach you all about them."

HURRICANES

Tropical Storms in Earth's Oceans

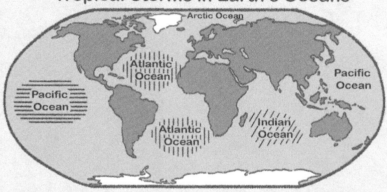

Arctic Ocean

Atlantic Ocean

Pacific Ocean

Pacific Ocean

Atlantic Ocean

Indian Ocean

Key:

Hurricane

Typhoon

Cyclone

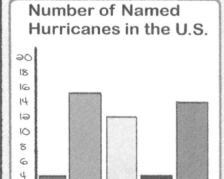

Number of Named Hurricanes in the U.S.

20 18 16 14 12 10 8 6 4 2

2000 2005 2010 2015 2020

Image of a Hurricane

By: Cosmo, Nova, Neb, and Cometta

Freaky Facts

- 1st named storm in US (Hurricane George hit Miami Beach, Fl in 1947)
- Biggest storm (Typhoon Tip at 1,380 miles in diameter, which is over 10 times bigger than the state of Florida)
- Strongest storm (Hurricane Yolanda which was a super typhoon with the highest winds recorded at 195 mph)

Hurricane Windspeeds

Category	Windspeed
1	74-95 mph
2	96-110 mph
3	111-129 mph
4	130-156 mph
5	157 and higher

How to Prepare

Create an emergency hurricane kit. Things to include:
- Bottled water
- Flashlight
- Battery powered fan
- Batteries
- Non perishable foods

Evacuation:
- If a meterologist has identified your town in a hurricane's path, your family may decide to evacuate. That means your family will pack, secure your home, and leave to stay in a safer location
- Remember to always have a plan for your pets and never leave them alone for a hurricane

The lesson had been a lesson that none of the 4th grade plutonians would soon forget. Newly gained information thrashed around the classroom like Category 5 strength winds. Cosmo glanced around the classroom as he filled with overflowing pride. His eyes twinkled as bright as the North Star as he looked out to the sea of concern that his classmates had created.

"Hurricanes like Hurricane Evan are life altering for the Earthlings who live along the coastline, such as Bonita Beach. The town they call home, once bright and filled with happiness, is in shambles. If you, my fellow classmates, are like Nova, Neb, and myself, your hearts are aching and wondering what we can do to help them. The Plutonian way is and always will be to help those in need. This weekend, we are hosting a field trip back to the beach where we will assist with a massive clean up and we need your help. Who's with us?"

The class was silent. The trio looked around at each other with worry filling their eyes. Seemingly all at once, their classmates shot their arms into the air, ready and wanting to volunteer with anything they could possibly do.

"We could bring homemade meals too! There's nothing better than warm plaple pie. Oh and $H2O$, we can collect gallons of $H2O$ and pass it out to the other volunteering humans! I know they'll be thirsty," rattled off Constella.

"What about clean clothes? We could collect fresh, clean clothes for all of the Earthlings who are still displaced from their homes," chimed Apollo, another classmate.

A single, silent tear welled in Professor Gorb's gigantic eyeball, getting caught in his monocle. "You, my wonderful students, are the kind of Plutonian I wish to be when I grow up," he sniffed. The class beamed with pride as they, as a class family, mapped out the plan for their philanthropic field trip to help restore happiness and normalcy to a hurting town.

With so much planned during their day in the learning room, time was ticking. The 4th grade field trip to the big blue and green planet was happening in t-3 days. With so much to do, the trio and their classmates wasted no time. Plans for clothing, $H2O$, and homemade food drives were in full force as the 4th graders plunged, antennae first, into action. If Plutonians are known for one thing, it's for caring about others, even those from another planet.

Chapter 8

October 8th, 2022

A golden sun on a shimmering sea and toasty warm sand. It truly was the picture perfect location that Cosmo had identified not long ago. Hundreds of beings, both Earthling and Plutonian, gathered on Bonita Beach ready to right what Hurricane Evan had so recently wronged. Volunteers were tackling an abundance of tasks all at once. Professor Gorb, who was in full Earthling camouflage along with the rest of the Plutonians, was in charge of distributing the refreshing H2O, clean and comfy clothes, and scrumptious homemade meals, courtesy of his 4th graders' tireless determination over the last few days. Eye brimming with pride as he soaked in all that Cosmo, Neb, and Nova had accomplished in such a short amount of time.

The collection and trashing of the scattered debris was led by none other than the trio's new friend, Sheriff, who to their surprise was actually named Bill. The three friends and Cometta were among those helping with Sheriff Bill's mission. Cosmo, Neb, Nova, and Cometta were in the middle of gathering dismantled fence posts near the shore line when seemingly out of nowhere something shimmering off the coast caught Cosmo's eye. Immediately he tossed his collection of broken fence posts into the sand and was sprinting towards the crystal blue water with Cometta closely behind him

"Cometta, activate Doggy Paddle," yelled Cosmo over his shoulder as he jumped into the sea.

"Aroo, activating Doggy Paddle," barked Cometta as her four legs suddenly transformed into propellers as she lunged for the glittering waves. Within seconds, Cometta was grasping the large reflective bobber. As she pulled, she realized that the bobber was connected to something far beneath the top of the water and that something was heavy. She pulled with all of her might. Cosmo finally caught up to her and together they were able to pull the mysterious box to the water's surface. Cosmo and Cometta began doggy paddling back to shore with the box secured to their side. Once Cosmo, Cometta, and the box made it back to where the water met the sand, Nova and Neb rushed to assist them. It took all of their combined strength to heave this monstrous box out of the ocean and into the sand.

Nova and Neb glanced at each other with confusion clearly in their eyes. Without so much as a whisper, Cosmo grabbed the secured latch that seemed to respond to his touch with a trickle of light that brought the box to life. A series of clinks and clanks, grinding gears, and a final ping that indicated that access had been granted. The latch popped open as the sides collapsed to the ground revealing the unharmed object inside.

"Is that…?" Neb started to question as he was cut off by a…

"YAHOOO!" wailed Cosmo with the intensity of a rocket blasting off for space. "Where…who…. how?!?" he continued as he glanced back to the shimmering ocean. As Cosmo looked, he found a family of Bottlenose dolphins breaching and splashing exactly where the reflective bobber had been. He swore that the littlest one waved a flipper at him as if to say "you're welcome!"

Inside the waterproof box, in perfect
condition, was Cosmo's missing Travel
Technology System that had been swept away
by the force of Hurricane Evan. Maybe it was a
coincidence. Maybe it was Bonita Beach's way
of saying 'thanks for helping me repair!'
Whatever it was, the trio and Cometta were
overjoyed.

CHAPTER 9

Though Operation 27 was technically a failure, the trio gained so much more than they ever thought. As a matter of fact, the three friends felt overwhelmingly proud of themselves for all the good they had done for the Earthlings of Bonita Beach. No matter how hard Cosmo tried to push away his Plutonian nature, it was clear to him, as well as everyone around him, that maybe he wasn't very diabolical but was indeed growing into a kind and inquisitive Plutonian afterall.

"Muahahaha, MUAHAHAHA! I am an utter genius!", hissed Cosmo as he cackled (convincingly diabolical), "I've got it! How could I not see this before?! This was NEVER the perfect location for our lair. There's way too much sand! No! We need something else. Something else ENTIRELY! We need snow... SNOW EVERYWHERE! The Earthlings won't know what hit them! Muahaha!".

Well... that didn't last very long.

Neb threw his massive arm around Cosmo's shoulders. "Annnnnddddd he's back ladies and gentlemen!" smirked Neb.

"Here we go again..." Nova mocked with a signature Nova eyeroll and an amused smile as she slid in under Neb's other arm. The trio turned back towards the hard working crowd of volunteers and simultaneously smiled toothy grins brighter than the North Star at the progress being made on the stretch of beach before them. Hurricane Evan may have wrecked this town, but the memories of the destruction were carried away with each full trash bag. It wasn't yet perfect and maybe it never would be the same as it once was, but with the help of both the Plutonians and the Earthlings, this once near perfect Bonita Beach was being rebuilt and would, one day, be better than ever.

Earth Invaders Operation 27 was written to represent the aftermath of Hurricane Ian that decimated Fort Myers Beach, FL in 2022.

Hurricane Ian Timeline

Sept. 23rd

Tropical Storm Ian first formed in the central Caribbean on September 23rd.

Sept. 26th

Ian strengthened into a hurricane on September 26th.

Sept. 28th

Ian intensified in the Gulf of Mexico and on September 28th, and became a Category 4 storm with maximum sustained winds of 155mph, just shy of a Category 5.

Ian made landfall near Cayo Costa, FL as the 5th strongest hurricane to strike the United States and brought intense winds, heavy rainfall, and catastrophic storm surges (12-18 feet).

Sept. 29th

After landfall, on September 29th, Ian downgraded to a tropical storm as it crossed the Florida Peninsula.

Sept. 30th

After crossing Florida, Ian reentered the open ocean and strengthened back into a Category 1 hurricane on September 30th, before turning and making landfall in South Carolina.

Oct. 1st

Ian dissipated over southern Virginia late on October 1st.

Bibliography

"10 Facts about Hurricanes!" *National Geographic Kids*, 15 Aug. 2012, www.natgeokids.com/uk/discover/geography/physical-geography/hurricanes/. Accessed 3 Sept. 2023.

"Hurricane Ian's Path of Destruction." *National Environmental Satellite, Data, and Information Service*, 4 Oct. 2022, www.nesdis.noaa.gov/news/hurricane-ians-path-of-destruction. Accessed 3 Sept. 2023.

"What Are Hurricanes?" *NASA*, 3 Sept. 2014, www.nasa.gov/audience/forstudents/k-4/stories/nasa-knows/what-are-hurricanes-k4.html. Accessed 3 Sept. 2023.

EARTH INVADERS
Operation 27

Made in the USA
Monee, IL
30 September 2023

43707251R10046